This Bk belongs to

. . . .

www.boxerbooks.com

For Ava & Edward - S.P-H. xx

To Fin and Maia - S.B.

First published in hardback in Great Britain in 2015 by Boxer Books Limited.
First published in paperback in Great Britain in 2016 by Boxer Books Limited.
www.boxerbooks.com

Boxer® is a registered trademark of Boxer Books Limited.

Text copyright © 2015 Smriti Prasadam-Halls
Illustrations copyright © 2015 Sebastien Braun
The right of Smriti Prasadam-Halls to be identified as the author and
Sebastien Braun as the illustrator of this work has been asserted by them
in accordance with the Copyright, Designs and Patents Act, 1988.

The illustrations were prepared using soft pencil and watercolour paint on hot press paper.
The text is set in Family Dog

ISBN 978-1-910126-84-4

1 3 5 7 9 10 8 6 4 2

Printed in China

All of our papers are sourced from managed forests and renewable resources.

Twit-to-Who?

Written by
Smriti Prasadam-Halls

Illustrated by
Sebastien Braun

Boxer Books

"Twit-to-woo," hoots the owl.
"Twit-to-woo!"
"Twit-to-woo?" says the sky.
"Twit to **WHO**?"

"To the animals at the farm, twit-to-woo. Twit-to-QUACK, twit-to-BAA, twit-to-MOO!"

"Twit-to-woo," hoots the owl.
"Twit-to-woo!"

"Twit-to-woo?" toots the town.
"Twit to **WHO?**"

"To the bus and car and train,
twit-to-woo.
Twit-to-BEEP,
twit-to-HONK,
twit-to-CHOO!"

"Twit-to-woo," hoots the owl.
"Twit-to-woo!"
"Twit-to-woo?" sways the tree.
"Twit to WHO?"

"To the babies
in the bath,
twit-to-woo.

Twit-to-AHHH,
twit-to-OOH,
twit-to-COO!"

"Twit-to-woo," hoots the owl.
"Twit-to-woo!"
"Twit-to-woo?" says the house.
"Twit to WHO?"

"To the children playing games,
twit-to-woo.
Twit-to-hide,
twit-to-seek,
twit-to-BOO!"

"Twit-to-woo," hoots the owl.
"Twit-to-woo!"

"Twit-to-woo?" sighs the sun.
"Twit to WHO?"

"To the evening sky,
twit-to-woo.
Twit-to-pink,
twit-to-red,
twit-to-BLUE."

"Twit-to-woo,"
hoots the owl.
"Twit-to-woo!"
"Twit-to-woo?"
murmurs the moon.
"Twit to **WHO?**"

"To the world
going to sleep,
twit-to-woo.

Twit-to-me,
twit-to-them,
twit-to-YOU!"

More Boxer Books to enjoy

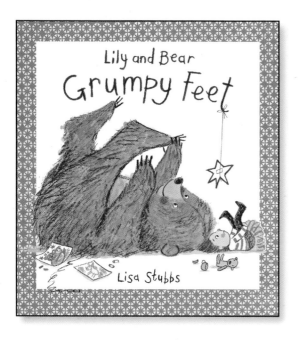

Lily and Bear: Grumpy Feet
by Lisa Stubbs

Something is not right. The day is too rainy, the teapot too dribbly and Lily's sunshine colour is missing from her crayons. Oh no, she's woken up with Grumpy Feet! What can her best friend Bear do to turn the grumps back into the jumps?

How Much Does a Ladybird Weigh?
by Alison Limentani

Have you ever wondered how much a ladybird weighs? What about the weight of a snail? A bird or even a swan? An extraordinary and original picture book which introduces you to a fascinating world of numbers, weight and wildlife.

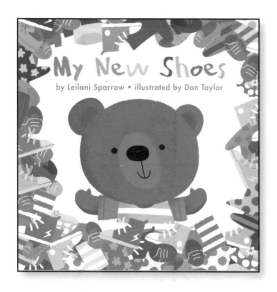

My New Shoes
by Leilani Sparrow
Illustrated by Dan Taylor

A simple introduction to buying a new pair of shoes. Short, fun and effective text with lots of rhythm and adorable animal characters to share the experience.